# The Scaredy-Ca

## By Roz Rosenbluth
## Illustrated by Deborah Borgo

© 1993 McClanahan Book Company, Inc. All rights reserved.
Published by McClanahan Book Company, Inc.
23 West 26th Street, New York, NY 10010

Printed in the U.S.A.

ISBN 1-56293-352-3

Mother Cat has two kittens. Herbie is curious and brave. But his sister Sarah is afraid of everything.

When Mother Cat and her kittens go for a walk, Herbie chases the mice in the field, but Sarah shivers when she sees them and stays right behind her mother.

"Scaredy-Cat," the mice squeak as she tiptoes by.

Herbie chases the birds until they fly up into the trees. But Sarah is afraid of them.

"Scaredy-Cat," the birds chirp as she hides behind Mother Cat.

Herbie is not even afraid of Mrs. Riley's dog Hector. But Sarah is very frightened.

"He is so big and has such big teeth," she whispers as they walk past him.

"Scaredy-Cat," barks Hector.

Sarah is even afraid of her own shadow.

"What is that black thing walking behind me?" she asks timidly.

"That is only your shadow," Herbie says kindly. "You should not be afraid of your own shadow."

Mother Cat shakes her head.
"What children I have," she meows.
"One is too curious and not careful enough.
And the other is afraid of everything."

One day, in the late afternoon, Mother Cat lies down for a nap. But Herbie and Sarah are not sleepy.

After a while Herbie says, "Why don't you come for a walk with me, Sarah. We can be back by the time Mother wakes up."

Sarah curls against Mother Cat's back.

"I feel safe next to Mother," she says.

"Oh, come on," says Herbie. "I will take care of you. And it will be fun. Who knows what we will find."

Sarah loves her brother and wants to make him happy. He is so brave, she thinks. I will be okay. So even though she is afraid, she gets up and puts on her hat and starts walking behind Herbie.

First they come to the field where the mice live.
The mice run when they see Herbie, but when
they are a safe distance away, they squeak at
Sarah, "Scaredy-Cat, Scaredy-Cat."

"Let's go home," meows Sarah softly.

"Stop that or you will be
sorry," says Herbie to the
mice and they stop their
squeaking.

The kittens walk into the
woods where the birds are sitting
on low branches. They fly away
when they see Herbie.

"Scaredy-Cat, Scaredy-Cat,"
they chirp at Sarah from high
up in the trees.

"Let's go home," meows
Sarah again.

"Stop that or you will be sorry,"
says Herbie to the birds and they
stop their chirping.

Soon the kittens meet Mrs. Riley walking Hector.
"Scaredy-Cat," barks Hector, and Sarah shrinks
against her brother.

"Please let's go home," meows Sarah.

"Stop that," says Herbie to the dog with a little
hiss. Hector stops barking and only growls a
little as they go by.

After a while Herbie and Sarah come to a neighborhood where they have never been before. Herbie sees a clump of bushes.

"There is something moving in there," he says. "I will see what it is."

And even though they are briar bushes, he pokes his little head into them, then takes it out quickly.  His back goes up.

"There is something black in there," he whispers to Sarah. "Something with a white stripe running down its back."

Suddenly, a skunk comes out of the bushes and stares at them.

"What is it," asks Sarah, shaking.

"I don't know, but I think we should get out of here," says Herbie and he turns to go.

But his pants are caught in the briars. He twists and turns, but he cannot get free. Sarah tries to help, but she cannot get him free either.

"Go and get Mother," says Herbie with a little quiver in his voice.

Sarah has never seen her brother afraid before. "I must get him help", she thinks, and she starts running home as fast as she can. She runs past Mrs. Riley and Hector, but she does not think of being frightened.

"My goodness", says Hector. "I've never seen you run before," and he stands back to let her pass.

She runs into the woods where she startles the birds.

"Why are you running?" they chirp, swooping down around her. But Sarah has no time to be afraid.

She runs through the field and the mice scamper out of her way.

"We have never seen you out alone," they squeak.

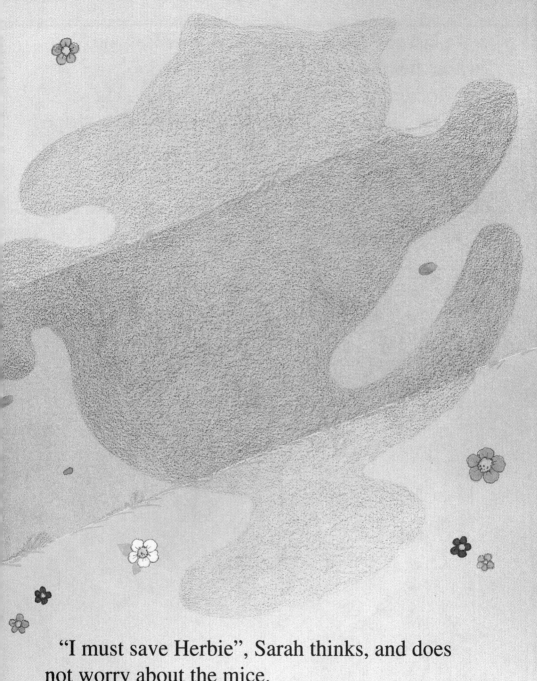

"I must save Herbie", Sarah thinks, and does
not worry about the mice.

She does not even worry about her shadow
running along in back of her.

At last she comes home to Mother Cat and wakes her up.

"Mother, mother," she cries. "Herbie is in trouble. There is a black thing with a white stripe staring at him."

"Oh, dear. A skunk," says Mother Cat. "Lead the way."

Sarah runs ahead of Mother Cat—through the field with mice, through the woods with birds, past Mrs. Riley and Hector, and with her shadow right in back of her. But she is not afraid of any of them. She is only afraid they will be too late to save Herbie.

When they reach the clump of bushes, Herbie and the skunk are still staring at each other. Mother Cat hisses and yowls and threatens with her claws. The skunk retreats into the bushes.

"Well," says Mother Cat, taking the briars off Herbie's pants one by one, "you would have smelled pretty awful if that skunk had sprayed you. You can thank Sarah for saving you from that. I am proud of you, Sarah, for being brave enough to come and get me."

Sarah is happy. She knows she is not everyday brave like Herbie, but she also knows that when there is trouble, she can put her fears aside and get help. And no one calls her "Scaredy-Cat" anymore.